Beast Quest

A TO Z OF BEASTS

ORCHARD BOOKS
First published in 2015
This updated edition published in 2020

A CIP catalogue record for this book is available from the British Library.

5 7 9 10 8 6 4

ISBN 978 1 40836 073 6

Printed in China

The paper and board used in this book are made from wood
from responsible sources.

Orchard Books
An imprint of Hachette Children's Group
Part of The Watts Publishing Group Limited
Carmelite House
50 Victoria Embankment
London EC4Y 0DZ

An Hachette UK Company

www.hachette.co.uk
www.beastquest.co.uk

Beast Quest

A to Z of Beasts

ORCHARD

CONTENTS

WELCOME TO AVANTIA!

IN THIS BOOK YOU'LL FIND FACTS, STATISTICS AND FASCINATING STORIES ABOUT ALL THE BEASTS TOM HAS TACKLED ON HIS BEAST QUESTS.

READ ON AND YOU TOO COULD BECOME

MASTER OF THE BEASTS!

ADURO

A

Wise old Aduro has long served King Hugo as the Wizard of Avantia. He is Tom's guide on his Beast Quests – his knowledge of Avantia's history and terrain, as well as the Beasts' weaknesses, has proved life-saving on many occasions.

7

GOOD

AGE	70
POWER	276
MAGIC LEVEL	192
FRIGHT FACTOR	65
SIZE	50

ALDROIM
THE SHAPE-SHIFTER

EVIL

Aldroim dwells in the network of secret tunnels that lie deep beneath Avantia. He is a four-legged, cat-like Beast, with eyes like burning coals and razor-sharp talons that can cut through rock. Aldroim's skin is made up of the feathers, scales, broken bones and hides of his victims.

8

0	AGE
234	POWER
179	MAGIC LEVEL
82	FRIGHT FACTOR
207	SIZE

AMICTUS

THE BUG QUEEN

A ncient scrolls found in Gwildor tell us that Amictus lays beautiful, shimmering eggs on the jungle floor. A highly protective mother, she guards her young fiercely, but will only attack with her poisoned claws and spiky limbs as a last resort.

GOOD

AGE	288
POWER	199
MAGIC LEVEL	189
FRIGHT FACTOR	92
SIZE	291

ANORET
THE FIRST BEAST

It is believed that this lizard-like creature was the very first to rampage through the kingdom of Avantia. Long ago a warlord stole the Beast's face and wore it as a mask – the "Mask of Death" – giving himself the power to control Anoret.

DANGER
DESTINY

Read Anoret's story in Beast Quest Special 12!

GOOD

Hundreds of years after this epic battle, Kensa the Witch sought to use the Mask to control not only the First Beast, but six young and innocent Beasts as well.

11

AGE	500+
POWER	296
MAGIC LEVEL	195
FRIGHT FACTOR	98
SIZE	460

A ARACHNID
THE KING OF SPIDERS

Arachnid lurks in caves near the village of Spindrel, in southern Avantia. He is a giant spider, capable of catching grown men in his webs and consuming them.

12

285	AGE
156	POWER
142	MAGIC LEVEL
78	FRIGHT FACTOR
255	SIZE

ARAX

THE SOUL STEALER

Arax was found in a cave in the mountain range of southwest Avantia. The Beast uses a long whip to snare his victims and steal their souls.

EVIL

13

AGE	271
POWER	242
MAGIC LEVEL	187
FRIGHT FACTOR	92
SIZE	125

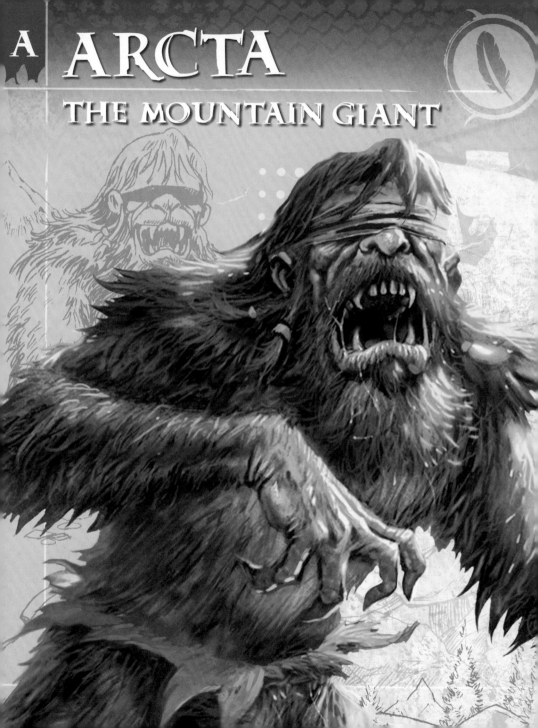

A ARCTA
THE MOUNTAIN GIANT

GOOD

Arcta is the last Cyclops of the Northern Mountains. These Beasts once dwelt at the top of the highest peaks, and protected the other mountain creatures. Like all Cyclopes, Arcta has only one eye. He is as tall as the pine forests that grow across the mountain slopes, with claws that can tear into chunks of rock.

15

DANGER DESTINY

Arcta gave Tom a magical feather, which allows him to float through the air.

AGE	324
POWER	132
MAGIC LEVEL	120
FRIGHT FACTOR	65
SIZE	480

BALISK

THE WATER SNAKE

One of the Beasts conjured by Sanpao the Pirate King, Balisk lurks in the Western Ocean. His long, powerful body is covered in tough scales and his fins have sharp claws. Dagger-sharp fangs fill his gaping mouth.

16

EVIL

Tom used one of Balisk's claws like a boomerang.

DANGER DESTINY

278	AGE
237	POWER
171	MAGIC LEVEL
90	FRIGHT FACTOR
333	SIZE

B BLAZE
THE ICE DRAGON

DANGER · DESTINY

Tom used his own shadow to defeat Blaze!

EVIL

Many hundreds of years ago, the whole of Avantia was covered in a sheet of ice. The Great Thaw restored life to the land, but for some parts of the realm, Blaze the Ice Dragon has unleashed a second Ice Age. Most dragons breathe fire, but from Blaze's jaws blasts a deadly stream of icy wind. The Beast freezes everything in his path – water, animals and plants. Nothing can escape.

19

AGE	313
POWER	210
MAGIC LEVEL	187
FRIGHT FACTOR	90
SIZE	320

BLOODBOAR

THE BURIED DOOM

Bloodboar is covered in plates of thick warty hide as tough as any armour. He towers over people but moves surprisingly quickly on short, powerful legs. If you're not crushed beneath his pounding hooves, you'll have to contend with his jutting yellow tusks. They're strong enough to rip houses to pieces with a shake of the Beast's head.

20

EVIL

233 AGE
350 POWER
180 MAGIC LEVEL
86 FRIGHT FACTOR
140 SIZE

21

DANGER ∞ DESTINY

Tom used a fragment of Bloodboar's armour as a deadly throwing star.

BRUTUS

THE HOUND OF HORROR

Brutus is a giant dog who hides in the fog of the marshlands of Henkrall. Some say he can actually turn into fog to evade capture or sneak up on his victims. He hovers in the air on huge leathery wings, which waft a suffocating stink. Brutus was made by the sorceress Kensa using the blood of Epos the Flame Bird.

0	AGE
285	POWER
189	MAGIC LEVEL
90	FRIGHT FACTOR
244	SIZE

EVIL

23

DANGER ~ DESTINY

In Henkrall,
all the Beasts
and people
can fly!

CARNIVORA

THE WINGED SCAVENGER

Carnivora is like a hyena but much larger, with jagged teeth and wicked yellow eyes that seem to ooze pus. Even on land she would be terrifying, but she can also fly! Carnivora's most lethal weapon is her fiery breath.

24

GOOD

293	AGE
250	POWER
180	MAGIC LEVEL
86	FRIGHT FACTOR
262	SIZE

25

DANGER DESTINY

Carnivora
can melt
frozen lakes,
making even the
landscape
deadly!

CLAW

THE GIANT MONKEY

Claw roams Avantia's Dark Jungle – a place where few dare to venture, and fewer still return alive. His chest is as wide as a horse is long, and his arms are thicker than most of the trees in the jungle. His eyes are a frightening shade of yellow, and he has gigantic clawed hands. But his deadliest weapon is his long tail, which ends in an extra claw.

26

465	AGE
217	POWER
134	MAGIC LEVEL
68	FRIGHT FACTOR
200	SIZE

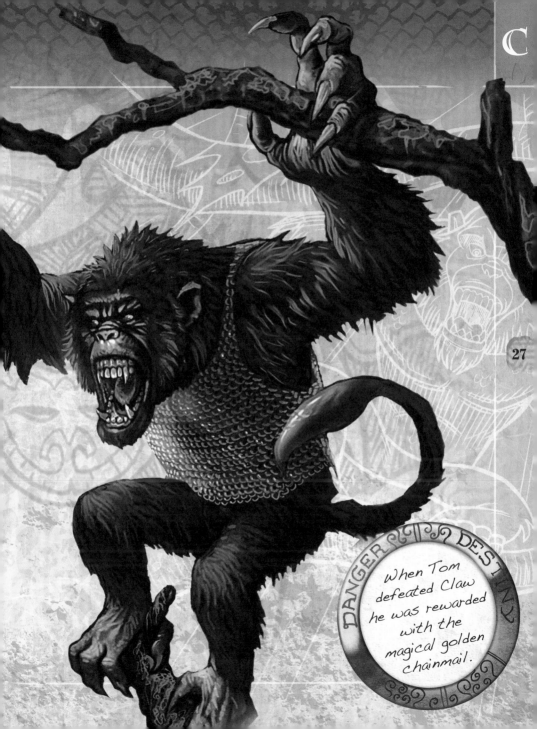

27

When Tom
defeated Claw
he was rewarded
with the
magical golden
chainmail.

DANGER · DESTINY

C CONVOL

THE COLD-BLOODED BRUTE

Convol is the largest desert lizard in the known realms. His back and tail are covered with ferocious spikes and his thick, scaly skin is almost impenetrable. His rotten teeth glisten in the desert sun, his body is covered with revolting warts and his gums are a sickening green.

28

300	AGE
230	POWER
171	MAGIC LEVEL
81	FRIGHT FACTOR
244	SIZE

GOOD

CORNIX

THE DEADLY TRICKSTER

At first, Cornix seems to be a beautiful woman with long dark hair, wrapped in a cloak of red velvet and carrying a lantern. But beneath her cloak is the rotting, feathered body of a crow. Her bird-like feet have vicious claws, and her face is a gruesome human skull. Cornix conjures strange lights to lure travellers. She then envelops them in her cloak – and consumes them.

29

AGE	0
POWER	209
MAGIC LEVEL	188
FRIGHT FACTOR	81
SIZE	104

C

CRETA

THE WINGED TERROR

This Beast is made of countless flying insects forming a column, which then sprouts arms and wings. Creta has terrifying fangs and two mighty horns.

EVIL

30

227	AGE
281	POWER
170	MAGIC LEVEL
90	FRIGHT FACTOR
290	SIZE

DALTEC

Daltec is a young wizard. Formerly Aduro's apprentice, he now aids Tom and Elenna on their Quests.

GOOD

AGE 21
POWER 252
MAGIC LEVEL 189
FRIGHT FACTOR 49
SIZE 50

DOOMSKULL

THE KING OF FEAR

Doomskull's most unnerving features are his eye sockets, which are completely empty. The Beast invades the nightmares of all who are unfortunate enough to gaze upon him. He looks like a lion made of stone, but up close, his victims can see his rippling muscles and sabre-tooth fangs.

EVIL

339 AGE
222 POWER
141 MAGIC LEVEL
83 FRIGHT FACTOR
150 SIZE

D

33

Tom became
Master of
the Beasts
after defeating
Doomskull!

DANGER · DESTINY

D DREDDA

THE TUNNELLING MENACE

Dredda's body is like a giant snake, and her diamond-tipped claws are deadly. Her teeth are powerful enough to chomp through stone and turn it to dust. Tom found a way to get the better of her by targeting the tiny patch of weak flesh on the underside of her jaw. Only a true hero of Avantia could tackle this Beast!

EVIL

3	AGE
264	POWER
148	MAGIC LEVEL
88	FRIGHT FACTOR
233	SIZE

DROGAN

THE JUNGLE MENACE

On his mission to reclaim his title as "Master of the Beasts", Tom had to undertake the Trial of Heroes – a Quest that few have survived… That is not surprising when its path is lined with Beasts like this huge ape. Drogan's jaws are full of ferocious fangs, and his eyes shine with pure fury…

EVIL

AGE	280
POWER	230
MAGIC LEVEL	67
FRIGHT FACTOR	82
SIZE	291

ELECTRO
THE STORM BIRD

In the land of Pyloris there dwell three Beasts, created when the legendary warrior known as Tanner defeated the Beast Krokol, turning him into three smaller creatures. This giant, metallic bird is a fearsome foe, whose surges of electric power are deadly during rain storms.

EVIL

391	AGE
282	POWER
154	MAGIC LEVEL
91	FRIGHT FACTOR
299	SIZE

ELENNA

Elenna is an expert archer whose arrows always strike true. She was brought up by her uncle Leo, a fisherman, after her parents died in a fire. Elenna has been by Tom's side since his first Beast Quest and is a loyal friend and brave fighter.

GOOD

AGE	12
POWER	56
MAGIC LEVEL	91
FRIGHT FACTOR	68
SIZE	38

ELKO

LORD OF THE SEA

Elko's mouth is lined with deadly fangs, and his hideous limbs can regenerate when severed by a blade. Elko was created by Kensa to wreak havoc on the kingdom of Henkrall.

EVIL

38

0	AGE
286	POWER
194	MAGIC LEVEL
91	FRIGHT FACTOR
287	SIZE

ELLIK
THE LIGHTNING HORROR

Ellik lurks in swampy water where she can remain hidden from her prey. Despite her thick body she can dart in the blink of an eye to snatch victims in her sharp fangs. Ellik's blue scales suck lightning from the sky and she stores the charge, ready to give her enemies a nasty shock!

GOOD

39

AGE	287
POWER	247
MAGIC LEVEL	177
FRIGHT FACTOR	85
SIZE	380

EPOS

THE FLAME BIRD

Epos, known to some as the Flame Bird, is one of the oldest Beasts in the Kingdom of Avantia. She is a phoenix who fears no injury or attack, because she can heal herself with fiery magic. Nobody knows exactly how many times this Beast has been reborn in the molten depths of the Stonewin Volcano, but while she guards it, the kingdom is safe from disaster.

GOOD

457	AGE
243	POWER
192	MAGIC LEVEL
92	FRIGHT FACTOR
240	SIZE

DANGER · DESTINY

One
of Tom's
treasures is
the healing talon
given to him
by Epos.

EQUINUS

THE SPIRIT HORSE

One of the most vile and dangerous of the Ghost-Beasts who dwell in the Forbidden Land is Equinus the Spirit Horse. His skeletal face is a mask of hatred and evil, frightening all wildlife in the Dead Jungle, where he has made his lair. When Equinus is in his ghostly form, it is possible to see the Beast's black heart.

EVIL

310	AGE
189	POWER
181	MAGIC LEVEL
85	FRIGHT FACTOR
148	SIZE

FALKOR
THE COILED TERROR

This vast, dark snake is one of the most ancient creatures ever to protect the kingdom, and a companion of Rufus, Avantia's First Wizard. But when he is bewitched by Berric, the venomous Beast poses a threat to the whole kingdom. Both his bite and his squeezing coils are killers.

DANGER · DESTINY

The Chronicles of Avantia have many tales of Falkor's heroics!

AGE	432
POWER	283
MAGIC LEVEL	168
FRIGHT FACTOR	83
SIZE	333

F FALRA
THE SNOW PHOENIX

This young white phoenix grew up in Rion, under the watchful eye of the Beast-Keeper Wilfred. Her wings ripple with flames, and her talons drip lava, but Falra is a sworn defender of Good now that Tom has freed her from Kensa's dark magic.

44

GOOD

6	AGE
240	POWER
155	MAGIC LEVEL
86	FRIGHT FACTOR
237	SIZE

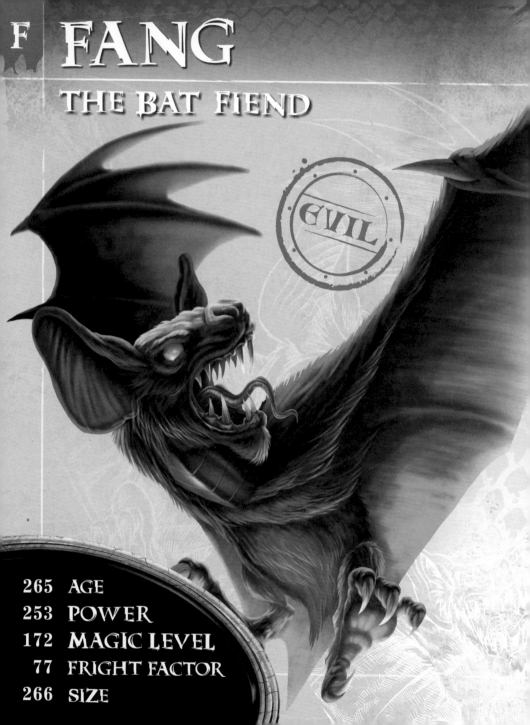

F FANG

THE BAT FIEND

EVIL

265	AGE
253	POWER
172	MAGIC LEVEL
77	FRIGHT FACTOR
266	SIZE

Fang lives in underground caves at the bottom of the Golden Valley of Kayonia. A giant bat with leathery wings like sails, Fang has dagger-sharp teeth and grasping claws which make him a deadly predator. When he's not in flight, Fang is almost impossible to spot in the darkness, but if you get too close to him you'll go blind!

47

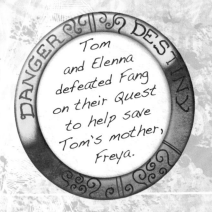

Tom and Elenna defeated Fang on their Quest to help save Tom's mother, Freya.

FERNO
THE FIRE DRAGON

In caves in the south, by Avantia's Winding River, lurks Ferno the Fire Dragon. Ferno is so enormous, he has been mistaken for one of the mountains. The Fire Dragon patrols the river and makes sure that the southern towns of the kingdom are never flooded. Should the waters rise, he can use his clawed feet to build protective dams. Their sudden appearances confuse the locals – but they are very grateful for them!

48

GOOD

288	AGE
212	POWER
180	MAGIC LEVEL
91	FRIGHT FACTOR
465	SIZE

F

DANGER   DESTINY

Ferno
gave Tom
a magical
dragon scale
for his
shield.

FERROK

THE IRON SOLDIER

This giant is formed from molten iron, and uses his sharp sword to magically draw flame into his body and increase his strength. The sword is not his only mode of attack – when Tom challenged the Beast, Ferrok conjured a net of fiery ropes to keep him subdued. The battle was one of Tom's deadliest ever!

50

DANGER DESTINY

Ferrok can enchant people and turn them into his servants.

217 AGE
293 POWER
180 MAGIC LEVEL
94 FRIGHT FACTOR
151 SIZE

51

EVIL

FLAYMAR
THE SCORCHED BLAZE

This terrifying monster is a Beast made of molten rock and flame, created in the image of the evil sorceress Kensa. Flaymar uses a whip of fire to attack her enemies and torment the people of Henkrall, and can turn herself into lava.

52

0	AGE
293	POWER
190	MAGIC LEVEL
91	FRIGHT FACTOR
122	SIZE

EVIL

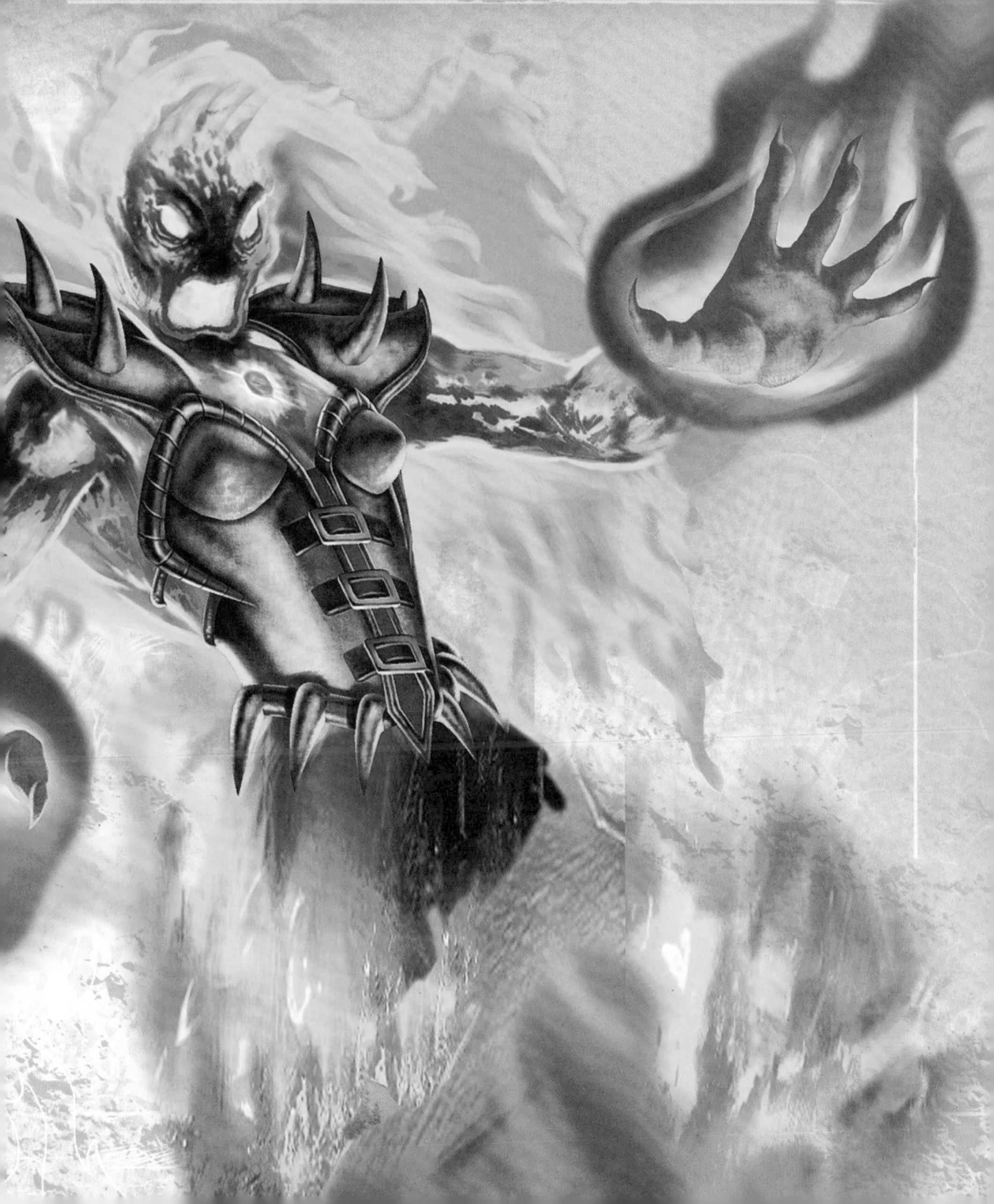

F

FLUGER

THE SIGHTLESS SLITHERER

In the twisting tunnels and waterways beneath Pyloris swims this long, slimy Beast, waiting to drag helpless Questers under the surface. He might be blind but he senses even the slightest movement in the dark currents of his lair.

54

EVIL

391 AGE
201 POWER
139 MAGIC LEVEL
95 FRIGHT FACTOR
317 SIZE

FREYA

A s deadly as she is beautiful, Freya first appeared as the evil wizard Velmal's companion. But it turned out that this mysterious woman was actually Tom's long-lost mother!

GOOD

55

AGE	44
POWER	190
MAGIC LEVEL	170
FRIGHT FACTOR	78
SIZE	51

GRASHKOR

THE BEAST GUARD

Grashkor was an evil Beast who killed a former Master of the Beasts. As a punishment he was sent by the Wizard Aduro to the Chamber of Pain, an island prison that floats in the stormy seas of the Western Ocean. There he guards the inmates, swooping over the battlements on leathery wings, and cracking his bone whip.

Look out for Grashkor in Series 15, when Tom and Elenna travel to Tangala...

56

257	AGE
289	POWER
150	MAGIC LEVEL
90	FRIGHT FACTOR
280	SIZE

GRYMON
THE BITING HORROR

Few Beasts are so ferocious, they wish they could bite the sun and make it dark... One such Beast is Grymon, who takes the form of a mountainous mole, vast and bulbous. His head narrows to a fleshy snout from which grows a pair of purple tendrils that Grymon uses to snatch and strangle his prey. His long fangs and single yellow eye strike despair into the hearts of any Quester facing him down.

57

EVIL

AGE	408
POWER	200
MAGIC LEVEL	116
FRIGHT FACTOR	94
SIZE	308

GRYPH

THE FEATHERED FIEND

In the Borderlands of Gwildor are four Beasts charged with the duty of protecting the Broken Star, a magical amulet of immense power. Beasts like this giant bird, her wings tipped with crystal blades, who will stop at nothing to keep it out of the hands of evildoers.

460	AGE
244	POWER
174	MAGIC LEVEL
90	FRIGHT FACTOR
262	SIZE

GOOD

H HAWKITE

ARROW OF THE AIR

Hawkite is an immense, fiery bird with glowing red eyes and razor-sharp talons. She is an agile flyer and can outmanoeuvre anyone who tries to attack Gwildor. Hawkite protects the land and its people.

GOOD

457	AGE
211	POWER
159	MAGIC LEVEL
89	FRIGHT FACTOR
260	SIZE

HECTON
THE BODY SNATCHER

Hecton is tall and bony with skin the colour of rotting flesh. He wears a cloak sewn together from scraps of fur and feathers, and a bull's head as a hood. He uses a net and a trident to trap his victims.

AGE	302
POWER	294
MAGIC LEVEL	188
FRIGHT FACTOR	96
SIZE	101

HELLION

THE FIERY FOE

This Beast's lair is deep in an active volcano. His body is like a column of flame, as tall as a blazing house. If he senses a threat, Hellion curls into a ball and rolls across the ground like a hurtling bonfire, scorching everything in his path.

GOOD

297	AGE
235	POWER
159	MAGIC LEVEL
82	FRIGHT FACTOR
132	SIZE

KING HUGO

Good King Hugo never planned to sit on Avantia's throne, but when his older brother died in battle, he was left with no choice. A kindly monarch who is loved by his people, he sent Tom on his first ever Beast Quest and Tom has served him loyally ever since.

63

GOOD

AGE	56
POWER	243
MAGIC LEVEL	40
FRIGHT FACTOR	70
SIZE	55

ISSRILLA

THE CREEPING MENACE

Issrilla is a mistress of disguise. This lizard Beast from the kingdom of Henkrall can blend into any background. Her skeleton is covered in jelly-flesh that changes colour, and she can sneak up on her enemies without being detected.

64

EVIL

DANGER DESTINY

Issrilla spits deadly acid venom that can burn flesh.

AGE 340
POWER 262
MAGIC LEVEL 193
FRIGHT FACTOR 93
SIZE 305

JAKARA
THE GHOST WARRIOR

Jakara is perhaps the most tragic Beast Tom has encountered. She is a hideous, magical fusion of the Ghost Beast Jalka and Kara, a former Mistress of the Beasts. When Aduro set off on his own Quest to find Kara, Tom followed.

66

DANGER ∙ DESTINY

Kara now rests in peace in the Gallery of Tombs.

60	AGE
296	POWER
185	MAGIC LEVEL
89	FRIGHT FACTOR
55	SIZE

He was
faced with
the task of
finding a way
to free the Good
Warrior from the
awful fate of being
bound to an
Evil Beast
for ever…

67

J JUROG
HAMMER OF THE JUNGLE

This gigantic, eight-limbed monkey-Beast can rip whole trees from the ground. His matted fur is purple in colour, and his jaws are lined with hideous, sharp teeth. His tail is tipped with a spiked mace made of precious redsteel.

68

EVIL

318	AGE
266	POWER
128	MAGIC LEVEL
89	FRIGHT FACTOR
298	SIZE

KAJIN

THE BEAST CATCHER

This Beast towers on two legs like a man, but has the body of a wolf, covered in a shaggy pelt. Under a snarling snout, sabre-like teeth can rip his prey to shreds. Kajin uses his powerful net to capture Beasts and people alike.

EVIL

399	AGE
243	POWER
152	MAGIC LEVEL
87	FRIGHT FACTOR
288	SIZE

KAMA

THE FACELESS BEAST

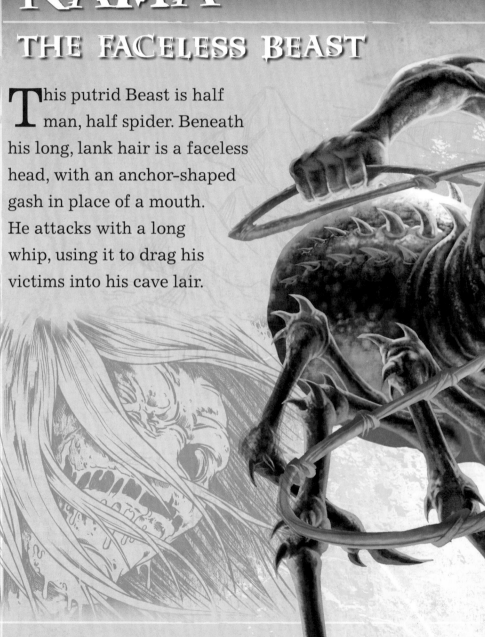

This putrid Beast is half man, half spider. Beneath his long, lank hair is a faceless head, with an anchor-shaped gash in place of a mouth. He attacks with a long whip, using it to drag his victims into his cave lair.

72

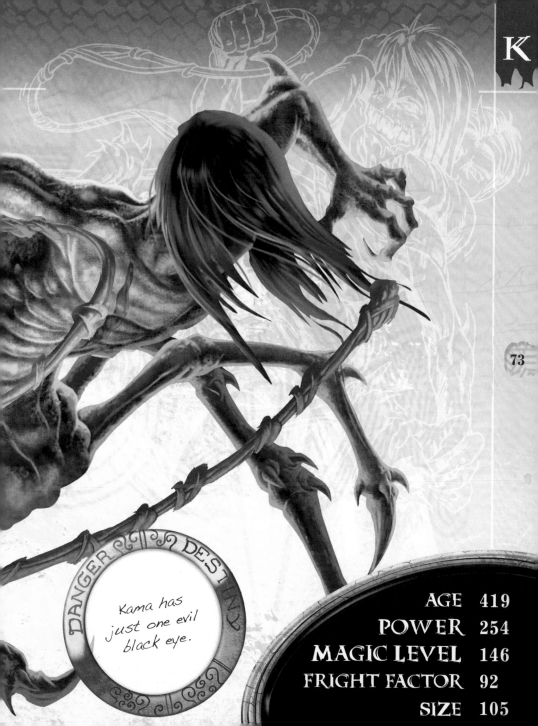

DANGER ✦ DESTINY

Kama has just one evil black eye.

AGE	419
POWER	254
MAGIC LEVEL	146
FRIGHT FACTOR	92
SIZE	105

KANIS

THE SHADOW HOUND

When the witch Kensa brought ordinary Gwildorian creatures under her thrall, she turned a gentle dog into this giant savage. Tom had to be very careful not to harm the innocent animal when battling the Beast.

4	AGE
231	POWER
106	MAGIC LEVEL
93	FRIGHT FACTOR
133	SIZE

K KARIXA

THE DIAMOND WARRIOR

This Beast of pure diamond was the last to be faced during the Trial of Heroes, and Tom was very fortunate that, by this point on the Quest, the warrior girl Amelia had gone from foe to friend. Otherwise, they might both have perished.

281 AGE

258 POWER

187 MAGIC LEVEL

83 FRIGHT FACTOR

159 SIZE

DANGER · DESTINY

One of Karixa's arms ends in a broadsword, fearsomely sharp.

KAYMON
THE GORGON HOUND

This gigantic dog can split her body for multiple deadly attacks. Kaymon lurks among the ruins of an ancient Gorgonian castle. Her huge paws can crush the bones of even the strongest warrior, and her massive jaws can swallow children whole. Avantia is lucky that this Beast has not yet found a way into the kingdom.

DANGER • DESTINY

Kaymon held Nanook the Snow Monster captive.

EVIL

K

79

AGE 296
POWER 239
MAGIC LEVEL 157
FRIGHT FACTOR 85
SIZE 152

KLAXA

THE ARMOURED ENEMY

Klaxa is twice as large as a rhinoceros. Many a warrior has been fooled into underestimating her as little more than a lumbering Beast. But Klaxa is cunning – she can retract her legs and head into her body so that, from a distance, she looks like a boulder. Then, when people wander past, she reveals herself and uses her poisonous horn to impale her victims.

232	AGE
210	POWER
179	MAGIC LEVEL
82	FRIGHT FACTOR
251	SIZE

EVIL

DANGER DESTINY

This Beast's hide is incredibly tough!

KOBA
GHOUL OF THE SHADOWS

At the end of the Warrior's Road Tom encountered this terrifying shape-shifter. His true form is of a muscular, genie-like Beast with huge clawed hands – but this ghoul delights in changing into other forms, to weaken the resolve of heroes and adventurers who cross his path.

82

EVIL

400	AGE
280	POWER
184	MAGIC LEVEL
93	FRIGHT FACTOR
140	SIZE

83

Koba's green eye became a powerful token of evil magic.

K KOLDO

THE ARCTIC WARRIOR

This spiky Beast is a giant made of ice. Despite his strength, Koldo is gentle – unless provoked by an enemy of Gwildor. There are rumours that the people of the kingdom have tried to capture Koldo, though it is difficult to believe anyone would be so foolhardy.

84

335 AGE
183 POWER
166 MAGIC LEVEL
84 FRIGHT FACTOR
115 SIZE

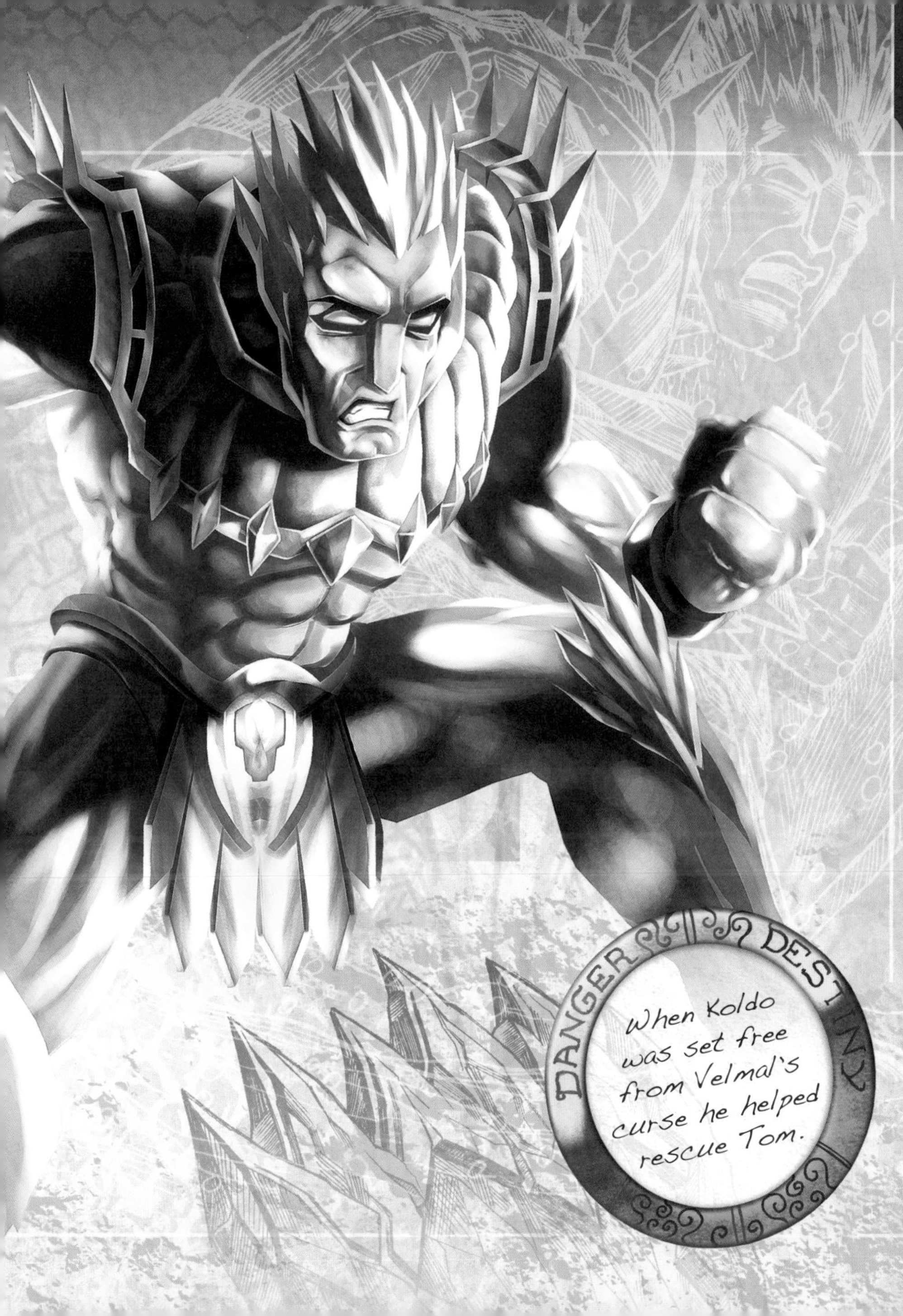

85

DANGER DESTINY

When Koldo was set free from Velmal's curse he helped rescue Tom.

KOMODO

THE LIZARD KING

This giant lizard lies in wait beneath the freezing black sand of the Icy Desert in Kayonia. When he senses footsteps, he breaks out from the dunes and attacks. Komodo's spiked head and slimy, forked tongue make him a terrifying sight, and he can heave his scaly body quickly over the sand using his stubby, clawed legs.

86

DANGER · DESTINY

Komodo has a hide as thick as chainmail.

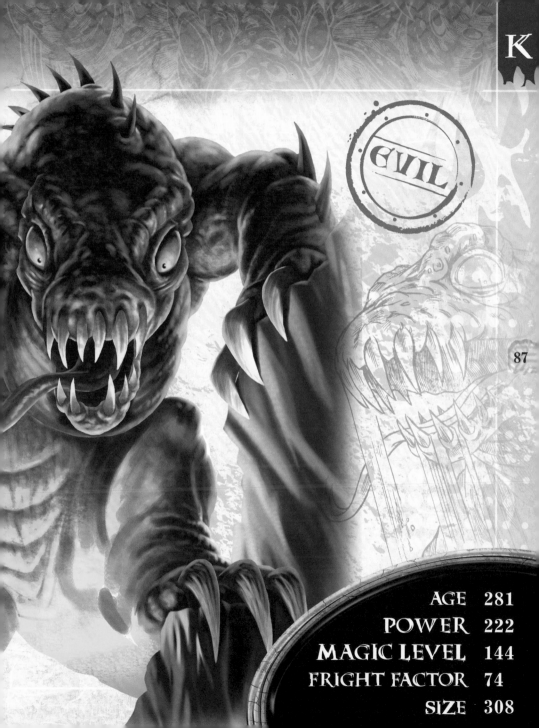

K

EVIL

87

AGE	281
POWER	222
MAGIC LEVEL	144
FRIGHT FACTOR	74
SIZE	308

KORAKA

THE WINGED ASSASSIN

With her scaly legs, huge wings and fearsome talons, it would be easy to dismiss Koraka as a lumbering animal. But she is clever enough to carry a spear as well, giving her several options for attack. Koraka was once a good, innocent shepherdess, but the witch Petra used her magic to turn Koraka evil.

88

DANGER DESTINY

Tom defeated Koraka with help from flocks of birds.

25	AGE
260	POWER
167	MAGIC LEVEL
93	FRIGHT FACTOR
101	SIZE

KORON

JAWS OF DEATH

This Beast is well named: hidden behind his black lips are teeth like daggers. Koron's muscular body is like a tiger's, and claws as sharp as the deadliest blade will tear your head from your shoulders. Most terrifying of all, he has a scorpion's tail that can dart forward as fast as a whip to attack his victims.

389	AGE
270	POWER
167	MAGIC LEVEL
94	FRIGHT FACTOR
119	SIZE

K

EVIL

91

Koron's fangs drip a burning spittle that nearly destroyed Tom's shield!

DANGER DESTINY

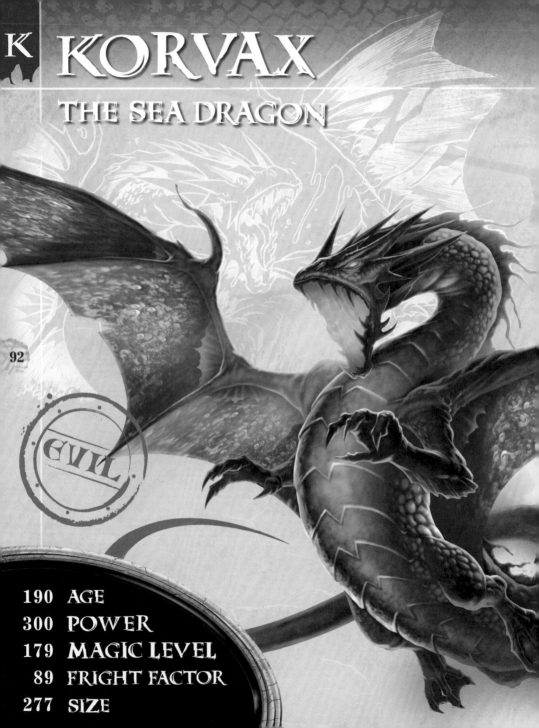

K KORVAX

THE SEA DRAGON

92

EVIL

190	AGE
300	POWER
179	MAGIC LEVEL
89	FRIGHT FACTOR
277	SIZE

In the frozen waters of Drakonia, "the Kingdom of Dragons," dwells Korvax – an ice-breathing Sea Dragon. As if that wasn't terrifying enough, her transparent body displays the poor sea creatures she has consumed. Questers must be very careful to avoid suffering the same fate!

DANGER • DESTINY

The only thing Korvax fears is fire.

KRABB

MASTER OF THE SEA

Krabb dwells in the ocean to the east of Gwildor. With a huge shell bristling with bony spikes, and six stabbing legs, Krabb protects the creatures of the sea. His armoured underbelly provides a home for many colonies of barnacles, and sea anemones cluster along his spiny back.

94

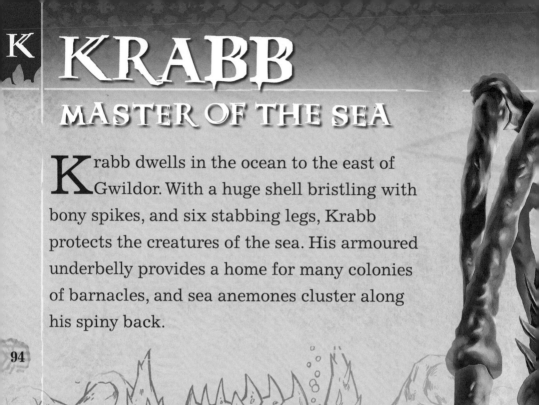

261	AGE
190	POWER
184	MAGIC LEVEL
88	FRIGHT FACTOR
277	SIZE

GOOD

DANGER DESTINY

Krabb saves food from his meals for his passengers.

KRAGOS AND KILDOR
THE TWO-HEADED DEMON

This two-headed Beast can change and re-form itself into different creatures. It last appeared in the form of a ram and a stag. The Two-Headed Demon desires the magical golden Cup of Life, a precious object which will protect anyone who drinks from it against death.

96

302	AGE
282	POWER
191	MAGIC LEVEL
91	FRIGHT FACTOR
140	SIZE

K

EVIL

DANGER · DESTINY

The Cup of
Life must be
kept in fire to
preserve its
magic.

KRESTOR

THE CRUSHING TERROR

This Beast has the neck of a serpent, coated in green scales, with powerful legs and webbed claws that propel him through the water. Krestor's red eyes can search out prey in the gloomiest depths. The Beast's snaking coils can squeeze the life out of his victims. His other deadly weapons are the jagged spines along his back. They can shoot acid strong enough to melt flesh and bone.

DANGER · DESTINY

Krestor's thick scales were too tough for Elenna's arrows.

98

313	AGE
240	POWER
167	MAGIC LEVEL
83	FRIGHT FACTOR
373	SIZE

EVIL

99

KROKOL

THE FATHER OF FEAR

This Beast posed the biggest ever threat to Avantia, for Krokol merged with Tom to wreak havoc – turning the kingdom's most honourable hero into a hulking warrior bent on destruction. Battling this Beast took Tom into a spiritual realm from which there was almost no return...

400	AGE
293	POWER
191	MAGIC LEVEL
96	FRIGHT FACTOR
188	SIZE

EVIL

DANGER DESTINY

Tom's ancestor Tanner battled the original Krokol.

KRONUS

THE CLAWED MENACE

K

An enormous vulture, this Beast's oily wings give out a dreadful stench and its beak opens wider than the tallest man. Beams of blinding red light burst from its glowing eyes, powerful enough to cut through stone. Its great claws can tear a person's throat out.

103

DANGER · DESTINY

Nanook the Snow Monster helped to defeat Kronus.

EVIL

AGE	313
POWER	280
MAGIC LEVEL	191
FRIGHT FACTOR	98
SIZE	307

KROTAX

THE TUSKED DESTROYER

Every year, one person from each tribe of the Wildlands, north of Avantia, is sacrificed to appease this terrifying mammoth. His great curved tusks are sharpened to scimitar edges, and iron spikes on his trunk make every toss of his head a potentially devastating strike.

103	AGE
257	POWER
162	MAGIC LEVEL
79	FRIGHT FACTOR
301	SIZE

KRYTOR
THE BLOOD BAT

K

Along the Trial of Heroes, Tom and Elenna did battle with this enormous bat-Beast, his fur the colour of blood, his razor-sharp talons capable of snatching up victims in an instant. The only way to defeat him is by using a magic flute, which emits a sound his sensitive ears cannot bear.

EVIL

105

AGE	279
POWER	249
MAGIC LEVEL	158
FRIGHT FACTOR	81
SIZE	259

KYRAX

THE METAL WARRIOR

This nearly invincible Beast of Henkrall – created by the wicked Igor, to do his destructive bidding – is brought to life by a drop of Tom's blood, and quickly becomes an menace Igor cannot control. So powerful is this warrior that Tom and Elenna needed to call Ferno for back-up!

0	AGE
209	POWER
161	MAGIC LEVEL
89	FRIGHT FACTOR
144	SIZE

LARNAK

THE SWARMING MENACE

This giant, locust-like Beast has six jointed legs and two pairs of wings. Her segmented body has a hard exoskeleton with arrow-like spines. Her feet secrete an oozing substance that traps her victims like glue, before Larnak wraps them in a cocoon until she is ready to devour them.

107

AGE	328
POWER	262
MAGIC LEVEL	153
FRIGHT FACTOR	95
SIZE	271

EVIL

UNCLE LEO

L

The fisherman who raised Elenna after her parents' death, Leo is a kind and honourable man, always ready to offer his niece and her best friend whatever support he can.

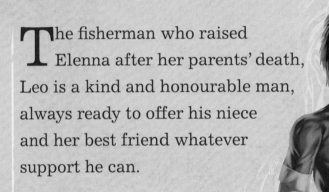

GOOD

54 AGE
74 POWER
20 MAGIC LEVEL
18 FRIGHT FACTOR
46 SIZE

LINKA

THE SKY CONQUEROR

At a distance, Linka might be mistaken for a sort of eagle, with her tawny feathers. But the Beast has no talons, or even feet. Her lower half is a feathered tail, covered in thick scales and ending in a stinger. By the time her victims can hear her shriek, it's too late for them.

AGE	390
POWER	249
MAGIC LEVEL	131
FRIGHT FACTOR	92
SIZE	250

LUNA

THE MOON WOLF

In the Forbidden Land's Dark Wood lurks Luna the Moon Wolf. Her claws are sharper than the deadliest of daggers, and her teeth can tear holes in any armour. But her most powerful and dangerous weapon is her ability to exert control over animals unlucky enough to be nearby.

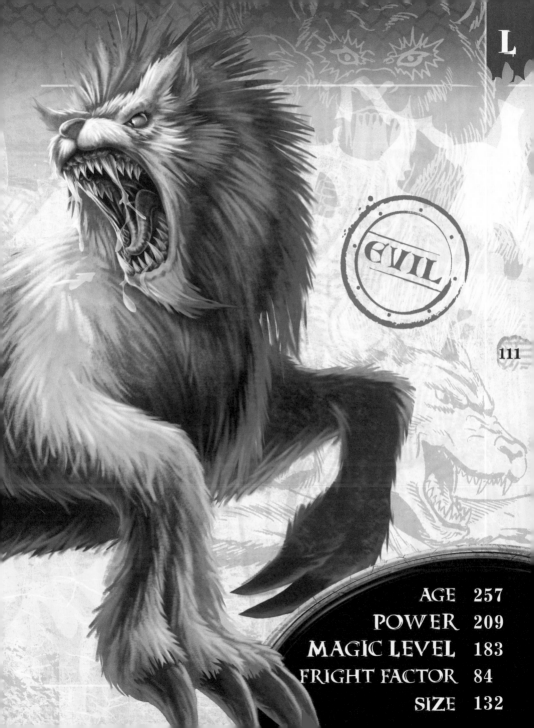

L

EVIL

111

AGE 257
POWER 209
MAGIC LEVEL 183
FRIGHT FACTOR 84
SIZE 132

LUSTOR

THE ACID DART

From his hiding place among the moss and rocks, Lustor emerges to reveal a toad-like face covered in warts. He has eyes like a fish and a long, curling tongue. Beneath his throat is a sac filled with a bright orange liquid that sprays in jets, burning through flesh.

112

328	AGE
235	POWER
159	MAGIC LEVEL
85	FRIGHT FACTOR
247	SIZE

LYPIDA

THE SHADOW FIEND

Lypida is a giant moth with mottled, browning wings that are tipped with savage-looking metallic hooks. A whip-like barbed tentacle can lash from Lypida's body as an additional weapon.

113

AGE	417
POWER	207
MAGIC LEVEL	148
FRIGHT FACTOR	88
SIZE	249

MADARA
THE MIDNIGHT WARRIOR

Madara is a giant cat who stalks the chilly mountains in the north of Tavania. Against the snow, she's almost invisible because of her crystal-white fur, and her lidless yellow eyes are always on the lookout for prey or danger.

GOOD

290	AGE
245	POWER
173	MAGIC LEVEL
84	FRIGHT FACTOR
256	SIZE

MAGROR
OGRE OF THE SWAMPS

This four-armed ogre, with a nest of snakes for hair and two sharp tusks, proved quite an adversary for Tom's father Taladon and the team of heroes who accompanied him. Arrows are useless against Magror's thick skin, and any Quester would be wise to avoid his club-like fists.

EVIL

AGE	117
POWER	265
MAGIC LEVEL	158
FRIGHT FACTOR	91
SIZE	300

AUNT MARIA AND UNCLE HENRY

Tom was brought up by his uncle and aunt in the village of Errinel, where Uncle Henry is a blacksmith and the village leader. He misses his relatives when he's away on a Quest, and especially longs for Aunt Maria's famous cherry pie!

116

GOOD

50	AGE
40	POWER
35	MAGIC LEVEL
40	FRIGHT FACTOR
52	SIZE

MARLIK
THE DROWNING TERROR

Some say Marlik is like a man, but with tentacles around his neck and green scales over his skin. Others say that his form is liquid, and he lies like a pool of stagnant water, waiting to drown unfortunate swimmers.

EVIL

AGE	258
POWER	232
MAGIC LEVEL	188
FRIGHT FACTOR	84
SIZE	120

MENOX

THE SABRE-TOOTHED TERROR

Anyone captured by the Pirates of Makai is at risk of being tossed into a pit to fight this gigantic rat, whose mangy fur gives off a terrible stench. His dagger-like tooth is as long as Tom's sword, and made of the same red metal as his cruel claws.

DANGER DESTINY

Tom defeated Menox in battle at the Redsteel Forge.

316	AGE
216	POWER
151	MAGIC LEVEL
84	FRIGHT FACTOR
189	SIZE

MINOS

THE DEMON BULL

Minos was once a calm and gentle bull who grazed the fields of Seraph. When Malvel's minion Petra fed him magically poisoned seeds, this kind creature transformed into the Demon Bull. Cruel spikes jutted from his hooves and twisted horns sprouted from his head and nose. They were sharp enough to tear a person to shreds.

GOOD

27	AGE
273	POWER
176	MAGIC LEVEL
97	FRIGHT FACTOR
295	SIZE

121

Minos blows a foul-smelling black steam out of his nostrils.

MIRKA

THE ICE HORSE

This dreadful Beast is terrifying enough, with his clawed hooves and sharp blue teeth. But even staying well back won't keep you safe – the Ice Horse's long tail is capable of shooting a hail of sharp shards with every whip and lash!

DANGER · DESTINY

Mirka is a terrifying combination of fire and ice.

123

EVIL

AGE	386
POWER	249
MAGIC LEVEL	188
FRIGHT FACTOR	90
SIZE	157

MORAX

THE WRECKING MENACE

This armoured brute can roll into a ball of interlocking plates and destroy anything in his path, and one flick of his blue tongue is enough to send a foe flying.

DANGER DESTINY

Even a forest fire and falling tree trunks could not stop this Beast!

EVIL

391	AGE
213	POWER
129	MAGIC LEVEL
85	FRIGHT FACTOR
305	SIZE

MORTAXE
THE SKELETON WARRIOR

Mortaxe resides in the Gallery of Tombs. In life, he was three times the height of a normal man, and the casket he lies in is one of the largest there. Although Mortaxe was once a brave warrior, he was turned to evil and held the power to control all the Good Beasts of Avantia.

358	AGE
280	POWER
180	MAGIC LEVEL
90	FRIGHT FACTOR
145	SIZE

DANGER ❧ DESTINY

The Gallery of Tombs is found down a long staircase lit with crystals.

MURK

THE SWAMP MAN

The Swamp Man lurks in the boggy Kayonian marshlands. Murk's body is made of mud and decaying plants, and his scalp bristles with flame. He waits beneath the surface of the dark waters, snatching any poor creature unfortunate enough to become stuck in the algae-filled sludge. Soon, only their bones remain.

128

DANGER DESTINY

Murk's power is reduced on dry land, away from the mud of the swamp.

EVIL

M

129

AGE 271
POWER 212
MAGIC LEVEL 181
FRIGHT FACTOR 87
SIZE 241

MURO

THE RAT MONSTER

With a body five times the size of a bull, the Rat Monster rampages through the fields of Kayonia. On dark nights, you might catch a glimpse of his yellow eyes gleaming between the cornstalks, or hear his horrible whistling squeak. His pink tail whips back and forth and his whiskers are as sharp as blades.

EVIL

300	AGE
243	POWER
156	MAGIC LEVEL
82	FRIGHT FACTOR
230	SIZE

M

131

DANGER ~ DESTINY

Tom defeated
Muro by
chopping off
his tail!

NANOOK
THE SNOW MONSTER

GOOD

N

One of Avantia's Good Beasts, Nanook's shaggy fur keeps her warm on the Icy Plains. She has piercing eyes and curved claws. The pounding of her massive feet can crack ice, though this loyal Beast does her best to protect this part of the kingdom.

133

DANGER · **DESTINY**

Nanook's bell forms part of Tom's shield and protects him from the cold.

AGE	335
POWER	165
MAGIC LEVEL	131
FRIGHT FACTOR	73
SIZE	265

NARGA

THE SEA MONSTER

This multi-headed sea Beast can terrify attackers into thinking they are dealing with several separate creatures. Its many eyes glow with fury, yellow and orange against its scaly skin. The stench of this Beast has been known to make grown men pass out in a dead faint.

346	AGE
233	POWER
146	MAGIC LEVEL
87	FRIGHT FACTOR
310	SIZE

EVIL

135

DANGER ✦ DESTINY

Tom uses Narga's jewel to give him perfect memory.

NERSEPHA
THE CURSED SIREN

Nersepha has the body of a woman and the tail of a sea-creature. Her dark scales shimmer like oil, and her green hair writhes like seaweed. Her red eyes cast an ominous glow underwater. Like the other Beasts of Makai, her body is enhanced with redsteel – in her case, a three-pronged dagger where her right hand should be...

DANGER DESTINY

Defeating Nersepha enabled Tom to foil Ria's plan to take over the land of Makai.

320	AGE
207	POWER
163	MAGIC LEVEL
95	FRIGHT FACTOR
168	SIZE

NIXA

THE DEATH BRINGER

Many people do not know they have crossed paths with Nixa until it is too late, for the Beast can adopt any disguise that she wishes. This is how she lures the nomads of the Dead Valley to their deaths. Nixa may be terrifying, but she does have a weakness: she cannot bear to look at her own hideous true form.

138

DANGER ✦ DESTINY

Nixa disguised herself as Elenna to trick Tom.

139

EVIL

AGE	259
POWER	208
MAGIC LEVEL	176
FRIGHT FACTOR	90
SIZE	160

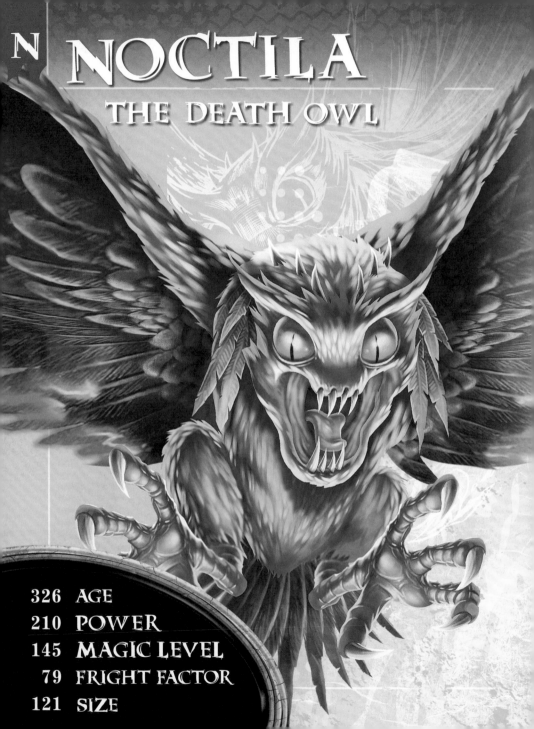

N NOCTILA

THE DEATH OWL

326	AGE
210	POWER
145	MAGIC LEVEL
79	FRIGHT FACTOR
121	SIZE

DANGER · DESTINY

Elenna helped Tom to lure Noctila into a massive net.

This Beast is like a giant owl, with burning orange eyes. His grey feathers drip with thick black tar that can burn a person's skin from their flesh. His beak opens to reveal jagged teeth as he sends out screeches that can deafen anyone nearby. His talons are deadly weapons and the gleam of evil can be seen in the black slits of his eyes.

141

EVIL

OKAWA

THE RIVER BEAST

EVIL

52	AGE
295	POWER
193	MAGIC LEVEL
97	FRIGHT FACTOR
110	SIZE

This mysterious monster was created by magic which infected a normal person, slowly transforming them into a Beast. Okawa is stronger than several men. His flesh is slimy sinew, and his back is protected by a hardened shell of green scales. Worst of all, his poisoned touch is enough to make you lose your mind, turning his victims into mindless slaves.

Okawa has only one weakness. If the hollow in the top of his skull goes dry, he loses his power. So keep him away from water, and you might stand a chance!

DANGER ~ DESTINY

An evil spell transformed Tom's uncle Henry into Okawa!

OKIRA

THE CRUSHER

The Isle of Ghosts is perhaps the most terrifying place Tom and Elenna's Quests ever took them, but it is also home to Good Beasts, like this colossal stone ogre. Okira is fiercely muscled, with fists big enough to punch through walls. The ogre's Good heart can tell the difference between friend and foe...if the friend survives his wild rage long enough!

144

88	AGE
217	POWER
138	MAGIC LEVEL
82	FRIGHT FACTOR
363	SIZE

GOOD

OKKO

THE SAND MONSTER

The desert people of Gwildor's Borderlands make offerings to this Good Beast formed from writhing, choking sand. He guards one of the fragments of the precious Broken Star, which he will yield only upon being defeated by a heroic warrior.

GOOD

AGE	430
POWER	246
MAGIC LEVEL	163
FRIGHT FACTOR	86
SIZE	301

OSPIRA

THE SAVAGE SORCERESS

One of Tom's most pitiable opponents, Ospira is actually the sister of Aduro, Avantia's greatest wizard, cursed to take the form of a dreadful Beast.

146

GOOD

28	AGE
271	POWER
196	MAGIC LEVEL
89	FRIGHT FACTOR
99	SIZE

DANGER DESTINY

Daltec
discovered
Ospira's journal,
which tells her
tragic story.

PLEXOR

THE RAGING REPTILE

Fishing communities in the kingdom of Tangala tell scary stories about the legendary "Cursed Fish", whose capture brought rains to help farmers. But no one actually believes the story, even though they hold an annual festival in which they capture a model version of the creature. They should not be so careless – for beneath the waters lurks Plexor, a monstrous reptile whose gaping mouth can swallow whole boats...and unlucky fisherfolk!

148

DANGER DESTINY

Plexor's glowing green eye is actually one of the Treasures of Tangala.

253	AGE
195	POWER
201	MAGIC LEVEL
85	FRIGHT FACTOR
291	SIZE

149

POLKAI

THE SHARK MAN

Before he was transformed into a Beast, Polkai was a man, the brother of Tom's enemy, Sanpao the Pirate King. Sanpao betrayed his brother, and cursed him to live his life as the Shark Man. Now, Polkai is one of the most terrifying Beasts in any kingdom – part man, part shark monster, he wields a poison-tipped cutlass that is even more deadly than his rows of jagged, vicious teeth.

150

DANGER DESTINY

The fin on Polkai's head is his only weak spot.

35	AGE
187	POWER
100	MAGIC LEVEL
83	FRIGHT FACTOR
102	SIZE

QUAGOS

THE ARMOURED BEETLE

One of the four ancient Beasts of Tangala, Quagos is a giant armoured beetle with the strength to burrow through the hardest earth and smash down walls. Her gleaming shell can withstand most blades, and her iridescent spikes can puncture flesh with ease. While the silver sceptre of Tangala is safe, Quagos cannot harm the kingdom.

152

302	AGE
294	POWER
179	MAGIC LEVEL
91	FRIGHT FACTOR
289	SIZE

EVIL

153

DANGER IN DESTINY

The silver
sceptre
protects
Tangala against
evil Beasts.

QUARG

THE STONE DRAGON

Watch out for this stone dragon's blue eyes – they have the power to turn Questers to stone! Is it any wonder that Tom's enemy, Berric, tried to bend this Beast to his will?

154

EVIL

265	AGE
269	POWER
178	MAGIC LEVEL
92	FRIGHT FACTOR
259	SIZE

QUERZOL
THE SWAMP MONSTER

The Wildlands are home to several Beasts, none more terrifying than this giant tree who emerges from the depths of a murky swamp. Querzol's branches stretch to ensnare its prey, whom it digests in its trunk. When threatened, it spits a cruel, flesh-searing acid. The only way to stop this dreadful Beast is to attack its amber heart, which is hidden at the bottom of the muddy swamp water. A Quester needs all their courage, and swimming skills, to prevail...

EVIL

AGE	97
POWER	219
MAGIC LEVEL	159
FRIGHT FACTOR	81
SIZE	254

RAFFKOR
THE STAMPEDING BULL

Raffkor, like the other young Beasts cared for by Wilfred the Beast-Keeper, grew up in the safety of Rion. He was a Good Beast, until he was turned evil by one of Kensa's wicked enchantments. Raffkor's mighty horns produce a magical blue fire that makes him a fearsome opponent.

156

DANGER · DESTINY

Tom returned Raffkor to goodness by cutting off his blackened horn.

R

157

GOOD

AGE 4
POWER 223
MAGIC LEVEL 181
FRIGHT FACTOR 85
SIZE 262

R RAKSHA

THE MIRROR DEMON

Raksha is not really one Beast, but several. He can only be summoned into the world under a strict set of conditions. First, it must be the height of summer, and second, he comes only from the Lake of Light, a hidden pool lying between the Forest of Fear and the Central Plains of Avantia. An enchanted Mirror lures other Good Beasts of Avantia to the Lake's edge, where Raksha can draw upon their combined powers.

158

257 AGE
292 POWER
200 MAGIC LEVEL
98 FRIGHT FACTOR
310 SIZE

EVIL

R

DANGER DESTINY

Raksha's armour is incredibly strong.

RASHOUK

THE CAVE TROLL

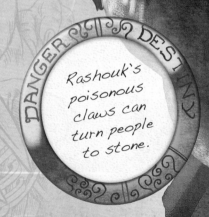

Rashouk lurks in the caves of the Dead Peaks, one of the most terrifying parts of the Forbidden Land. He is five times as wide as a man, and his powerful body makes him very dangerous. Rashouk does have one weakness – if a warrior can lure him into the open, he will have a chance to exploit Rashouk's fear of bright light. Sunshine, fire, lightning – all can be used as weapons against the Cave Troll.

321	AGE
165	POWER
154	MAGIC LEVEL
81	FRIGHT FACTOR
300	SIZE

DANGER · DESTINY

Rashouk's poisonous claws can turn people to stone.

161

EVIL

RAVIRA
RULER OF THE UNDERWORLD

Ravira rules the Underworld of Avantia. She lives in a castle made of glistening white stone, high above a city and surrounded by rivers of molten lava. She is guarded by the Hounds of Avantia, who can tear a person to shreds.

359	AGE
291	POWER
190	MAGIC LEVEL
91	FRIGHT FACTOR
98	SIZE

REPTUS

THE OCEAN KING

Little is known of this mysterious Beast, except that his body dwarfs most ships. Unscrupulous villains have tried to control him with a magical diamond which now lies at the bottom of the sea. All of Avantia prays that it stays there!

GOOD

AGE	311
POWER	177
MAGIC LEVEL	199
FRIGHT FACTOR	86
SIZE	304

ROKK

THE WALKING MOUNTAIN

Rokk lives in the mountains surrounding the town of Tion, in Gwildor. He can hide easily among the boulder-strewn slopes, because he is actually made of rocks – boulders form his huge, squat legs and arms, and a great slab of stone makes his chest. Rokk's eyes are deep chasms that seem to suck in the light.

164

DANGER DESTINY

Tom had to climb up into Rokk's eye sockets to defeat him!

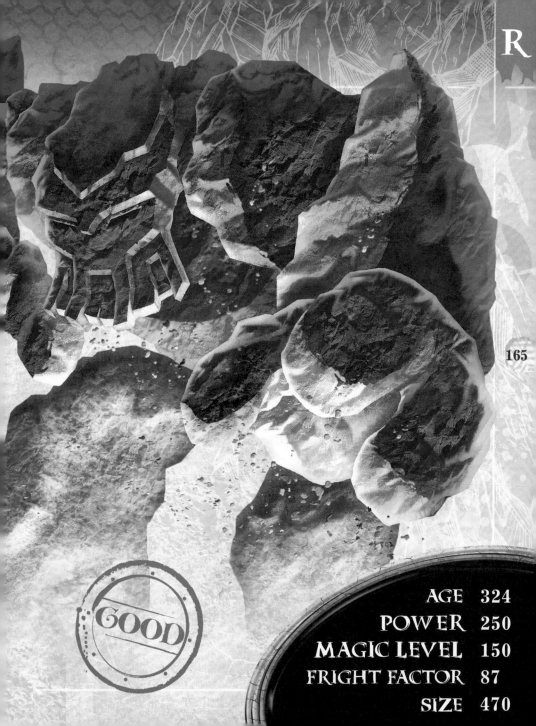

165

GOOD

AGE	324
POWER	250
MAGIC LEVEL	150
FRIGHT FACTOR	87
SIZE	470

R | RONAK

THE TOXIC TERROR

The wicked witch Kensa not only cursed an innocent ram to become a Beast who rampaged through Gwildor, but also poisoned his hooves so that every step he takes destroys soil and vegetation.

GOOD

7	AGE
24	POWER
111	MAGIC LEVEL
85	FRIGHT FACTOR
152	SIZE

RYKAR

THE FIRE HOUND

This giant dog is a terrifying opponent – get too close, and he can tear you to pieces with his cruel yellow teeth; keep your distance, and Rykar can pick you off with his fiery breath. A Quester must stay focused and alert to prevail against this Beast.

EVIL

167

AGE	186
POWER	261
MAGIC LEVEL	160
FRIGHT FACTOR	92
SIZE	193

SAUREX

THE SILENT CREEPER

The final guardian of the Broken Star, this giant lizard is made more deadly by his ability to camouflage himself, so that a Quester won't see him until it's very nearly too late!

GOOD

442	AGE
247	POWER
137	MAGIC LEVEL
91	FRIGHT FACTOR
290	SIZE

SCALAMANX

THE FIERY FURY

EVIL

Many years after Tom's mother, Freya, conquered this reptilian lava monster, Tom was drawn into a battle with it when his friend Petra accidentally restored it to life!

169

AGE	161
POWER	254
MAGIC LEVEL	180
FRIGHT FACTOR	89
SIZE	249

S | SEPRON

THE SEA SERPENT

Sepron guards the Western Ocean, keeping Avantia's fishing boats safe from storms and patrolling the depths right down to the sea bed. His eyes are pale and his body is covered in green scales that glimmer with every colour of the rainbow when the sun hits them.

170

DANGER ∙ DESTINY

Sepron can create tidal waves with a swish of his tail.

261	AGE
184	POWER
176	MAGIC LEVEL
83	FRIGHT FACTOR
300	SIZE

GOOD

SERPIO

THE SLITHERING SHADOW

Serpio has the body of a giant snake, with scales that gleam in the darkness. He was created by the sorceress Kensa using the blood of Arcta the Mountain Giant, and like that Beast, he has only one eye, which glows brightly. He can breathe a hail of freezing water, encasing his victims in ice.

172

0	AGE
284	POWER
180	MAGIC LEVEL
87	FRIGHT FACTOR
327	SIZE

EVIL

173

DANGER · DESTINY

Tom fought
Serpio in a dark
old mineshaft.

SHAMANI

THE RAGING FLAME

Shamani takes the form of a huge cat, with black fur that gleams like spilt oil. He can leap twenty paces in a single bound and he has long, vicious fangs. Shamani is an ancient Beast, once defeated by the Red Knight of Forton. This Beast's roars are so loud they splinter rocks, and sparks fly when he rakes his claws across the ground. With a flick of his tail, he can knock a grown man flying.

174

EVIL

330 AGE
220 POWER
155 MAGIC LEVEL
82 FRIGHT FACTOR
192 SIZE

DANGER · DESTINY

Shamani's claws are made of magical amber.

S SILVER

GOOD

When Elenna was a young girl, she injured herself in the woods and was rescued by a grey wolf, who let her sit on his back as he carried her home. She would go on to name the wolf Silver, and he has walked loyally by her side ever since.

176

35	AGE
147	POWER
34	MAGIC LEVEL
60	FRIGHT FACTOR
35	SIZE

SILVER

THE WILD TERROR

In the land of Seraph, the evil wizard Malvel used the Warlock's Staff to turn Silver into a terrifying Beast many times his usual size.

GOOD

AGE	35
POWER	270
MAGIC LEVEL	150
FRIGHT FACTOR	95
SIZE	237

SKALIX

THE SNAPPING HORROR

Skalix's broad, muscular body is armoured with black scales, and his teeth are as sharp as daggers. His tail ends in a great club, spiked with bony knives, making it difficult for a Quester to have any line of attack against this monstrous crocodile.

178

DANGER DESTINY

On this Quest, Tom had to prevent Malvel from seizing the Amulet of Avantia.

S

EVIL

179

AGE	173
POWER	228
MAGIC LEVEL	164
FRIGHT FACTOR	86
SIZE	246

SKOLO

THE BLADED MONSTER

I f it had not been for Avantia's ruler, King Hugo, being infected with the rare, deadly Skolodine poison, Tom would not have had to venture into the Darkmaw Caves in search of an antidote – and it is possible that this giant, steel-winged centipede Beast would have remained unseen in her lair for many, many years.

180

GOOD

Skolo uses a sticky purple goo to trap her victims.

392	AGE
285	POWER
183	MAGIC LEVEL
94	FRIGHT FACTOR
297	SIZE

181

SKOR

THE WINGED STALLION

Fear this creature! His long, yellowish teeth can tear chunks of human flesh, because they drip with acidic saliva. Silver sparks flash from his eyes and his wingtips scatter golden light. Don't be distracted by the shimmering colours, however – this Beast does not bleed, so he is unstoppable in battle. Even the deadliest blow will not wound Skor!

EVIL

183

Skor is a fearsome enemy both on land and in the air.

DANGER · DESTINY

AGE	264
POWER	221
MAGIC LEVEL	132
FRIGHT FACTOR	78
SIZE	160

SKRAR

THE NIGHT SCAVENGER

Skrar is a hulking, muscular Beast whose body is coated in spiky white fur that can burst into scorchingly hot purple flames. If that isn't terrifying enough, his smooth, scaled, serpent-like tail can knock his foes unconscious.

184

EVIL

429	AGE
251	POWER
176	MAGIC LEVEL
93	FRIGHT FACTOR
292	SIZE

185

The heat Skrar gave off during his battle with Tom caused a whole lake to evaporate!

SKURIK

THE FOREST DEMON

The repulsive, foul-smelling Forest Demon is one of the most frightening Beasts found along the Warrior's Road. This giant maggot-like creature steals children and traps his victims alive in sticky sacs hung from the trees in the woods near Tom's home village, Errinel.

186

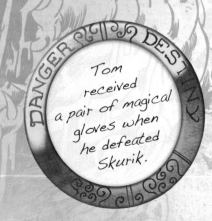

367	AGE
196	POWER
137	MAGIC LEVEL
91	FRIGHT FACTOR
304	SIZE

DANGER DESTINY

Tom received a pair of magical gloves when he defeated Skurik.

187

SLIVKA

THE COLD-HEARTED CURSE

Slivka dwells in the jungle, sliding between trees and shooting from the undergrowth in a flash. This giant lizard's muscular body is covered in blue scales. His tail can smash down trees, and his wide head is crested with jutting horns. Slivka can rise up on two rear legs, slashing with his claws, or whip out his long tongue to snatch his victims and draw them towards his sharp teeth.

DANGER · DESTINY

Tom and Elenna battled Slivka on the Warrior's Road.

EVIL

S

189

AGE	371
POWER	245
MAGIC LEVEL	130
FRIGHT FACTOR	90
SIZE	289

SOARA

THE STINGING SPECTRE

If you are brave enough to travel the seas around Corsair Island, it won't just be pirates that you must look out for. The waters are home to a colossal jellyfish Beast, whose swirling mass can create whirlpools, ready to snatch dinghies and ships that stray too close.

278 AGE

197 POWER

108 MAGIC LEVEL

91 FRIGHT FACTOR

306 SIZE

DANGER DESTINY

Tom faced
Soara as part
of the Trial
of Heroes.

SOLAK

SCOURGE OF THE SEA

Solak is a giant shark-like Beast, feared by even the bravest sailors. His sleek silvery body seems to change colour as he slides through the water, offering camouflage – first glowing blue, then indigo, then grey. His eyes stare with cold hatred upon his victims. He has several rows of teeth in his gaping mouth, trailing scraps of torn flesh, and his many fins are made of serrated bone.

192

EVIL

193

Tom used the blue Lightning Token to help him defeat Solak.

DANGER · DESTINY

AGE	399
POWER	256
MAGIC LEVEL	134
FRIGHT FACTOR	89
SIZE	330

SOLIX

THE DEADLY SWARM

Another Beast conjured by Kensa from innocent creatures, this time millions of helpless ants joined together to create one gigantic insect-Beast. Her only weakness is the sound made by the ram's horn Tom won on a previous Quest.

194

GOOD

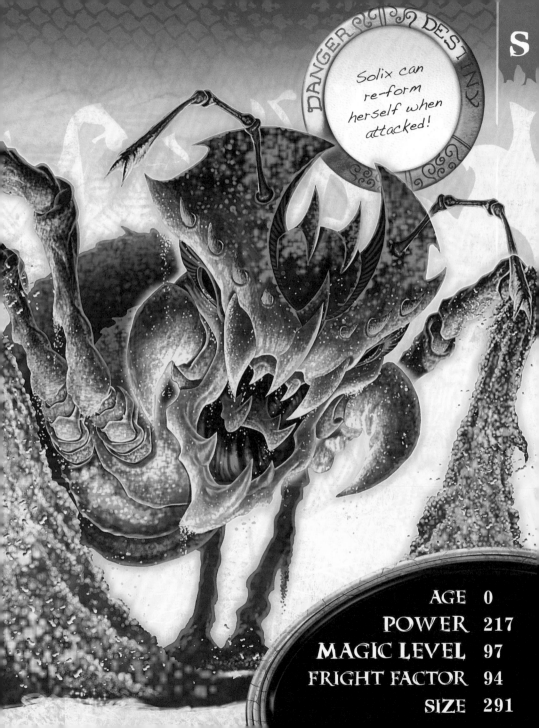

DANGER DESTINY

S

Solix can re-form herself when attacked!

AGE	0
POWER	217
MAGIC LEVEL	97
FRIGHT FACTOR	94
SIZE	291

S | SOLTRA

THE STONE CHARMER

Soltra stalks the misty marshes near Tom's village of Errinel. Her face glows milk-white like the full moon. Soltra appears beautiful and draws you nearer with her charms. But be careful! If you stare into her one eye for too long, your body will turn to stone…

196

487	AGE
196	POWER
184	MAGIC LEVEL
72	FRIGHT FACTOR
107	SIZE

EVIL

SPIKEFIN
THE WATER KING

Brenner, an innocent fisherman, was slashed by Malvel with a poisoned blade and drowned in the sea. He re-emerged as Spikefin: half man, half sea-creature. Spikefin's ferocious claws, razor-sharp fins and huge whipping tail can destroy any boat sailing in his path.

197

GOOD

AGE	39
POWER	250
MAGIC LEVEL	180
FRIGHT FACTOR	85
SIZE	220

S SPIROS

THE GHOST PHOENIX

Spiros is no ordinary phoenix. She is known as the lost Seventh Beast of Avantia. The Dark Wizard Malvel bewitched Spiros, separating her body from her soul, and now she lives between life and death. She is rarely seen in the skies over the kingdom, and no ordinary person can tame her.

198

GOOD

376	AGE
250	POWER
189	MAGIC LEVEL
89	FRIGHT FACTOR
235	SIZE

DANGER · DESTINY

Spiros has the rare power of All-Sight.

STEALTH

THE GHOST PANTHER

All the known kingdoms dread Stealth. He has a panther's lithe grace, and three tails that he can use to snatch up his enemies, tossing them into his mouth like morsels of food. Even a warrior who escaped those tails would be at the mercy of his deadly teeth and giant claws.

EVIL

201

DANGER DESTINY

One scratch from Stealth's claws can turn his victims evil!

AGE	243
POWER	199
MAGIC LEVEL	150
FRIGHT FACTOR	89
SIZE	155

STING

THE SCORPION MAN

Sting was created by the Dark Wizard Malvel. The Beast lived in the terrifying, dark tunnels beneath Malvel's Gorgonian castle. Tom and Elenna were attacked by Sting's giant pincers in a crumbling chamber, from which they only just managed to escape!

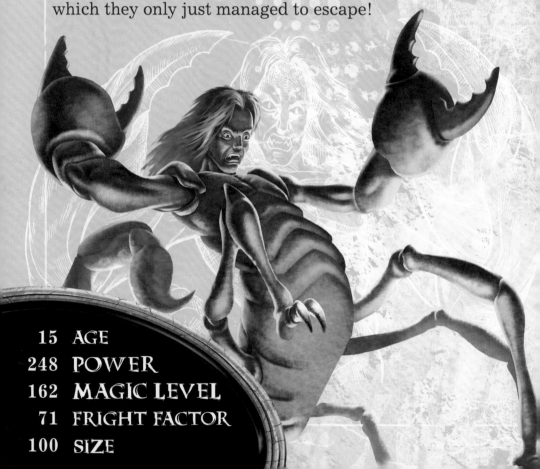

15	AGE
248	POWER
162	MAGIC LEVEL
71	FRIGHT FACTOR
100	SIZE

STORM

GOOD

Storm was born in King Hugo's stables, and at first he was nervous and jumpy. Fortunately, the wizard Aduro realised that Storm had an important role to play in Avantia's future and that Tom was his true master. Storm can gallop long distances without tiring.

203

AGE	15
POWER	200
MAGIC LEVEL	89
FRIGHT FACTOR	50
SIZE	60

S | STRYTOR

THE SKELETON DRAGON

This Beast forms himself out of a pile of bones, right before Tom and Elenna's eyes. He takes the form of a vast skeletal dragon, glowing a hideous white against the night sky. Questers can see his fiery breath forming in his hollow belly, but are usually powerless to save themselves from his blasts...

301	AGE
282	POWER
188	MAGIC LEVEL
94	FRIGHT FACTOR
326	SIZE

STYRO

THE SNAPPING BRUTE

This lobster is bewitched to become the size of a whale, and far more formidable – filled with such rage that Tom can barely handle the sound of this Beast's voice.

GOOD

205

AGE	17
POWER	203
MAGIC LEVEL	174
FRIGHT FACTOR	90
SIZE	292

T TAGUS
THE HORSE-MAN

GOOD

Tagus the Horse-Man patrols the Central Plains of Avantia, guarding cattle from hyenas and wolves. He has the torso of a man, but the body of a powerful stallion. Though small compared to the other Good Beasts of Avantia, he towers over normal men and can gallop faster than any horse.

406	AGE
73	POWER
114	MAGIC LEVEL
58	FRIGHT FACTOR
100	SIZE

TALADON

Tom's father, Taladon, was once a boy knight who set off on a Quest of his own to discover more about Avantia's Beasts. A brave warrior, he became Master of the Beasts. Now Taladon's Golden Armour has been passed on to his son, Tom, the new Master of the Beasts.

207

GOOD

AGE	48
POWER	201
MAGIC LEVEL	176
FRIGHT FACTOR	80
SIZE	55

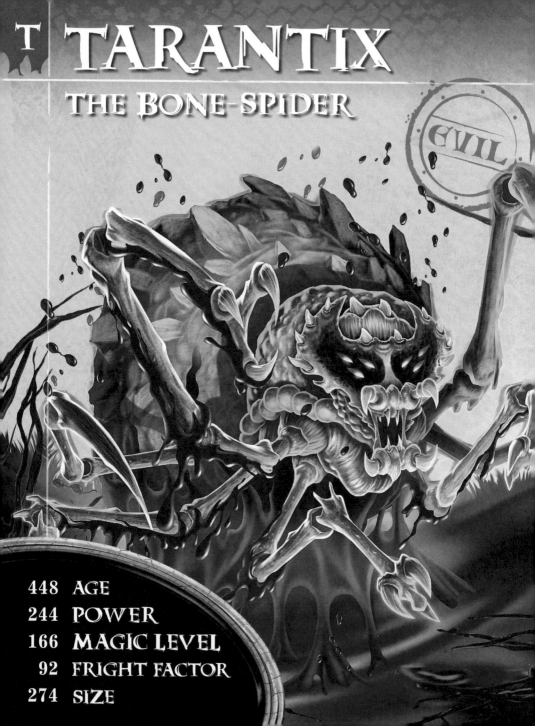

T TARANTIX
THE BONE-SPIDER

EVIL

448 AGE
244 POWER
166 MAGIC LEVEL
92 FRIGHT FACTOR
274 SIZE

Tarantix is a monstrous spider the size of a
stagecoach. Six of her legs end in a three-toed
claw, and her massive body is covered by pockmarked,
greying bone. A tapered point at the rear end of the
Beast's abdomen generates gooey spider silk, and the
many eyes clustered on her vast head glitter with
venomous hatred.

209

DANGER DESTINY

Tarantix
burrows
underneath the
desert sands to
evade Tom.

TARGRO

THE ARCTIC MENACE

Targro prowls the icy wasteland, his pale lilac fur helping him blend in with the snow. Sniffing the air with a pointed snout, he searches for any traveller foolish enough to be lost in the snow. If you're lucky, you might hear the creak of his clawed feet dipping in and out of the drifts, but more likely the first and last thing you'll know is the stink of his rotting breath.

210

370	AGE
232	POWER
134	MAGIC LEVEL
89	FRIGHT FACTOR
268	SIZE

Tom used one of Targro's claws to help defeat Slivka.

211

EVIL

DANGER DESTINY

T

TARROK
THE BLOOD SPIKE

EVIL

212

A dreadful Beast created by the witch Kensa, Tarrok brings fear to the desert in the west of Henkrall, flinging a hideous yellow sap that encases his victims in a ghastly cocoon. His muscular body is covered with cruel red spikes that can repel even the bravest of warriors.

213

DANGER DESTINY

Tarrok is like a monstrous cactus with his spines and sap.

AGE	0
POWER	287
MAGIC LEVEL	150
FRIGHT FACTOR	89
SIZE	268

TAURON

THE POUNDING FURY

This horrifying "buffalo-man" was created by Kensa the Witch from the blood of Tagus, Avantia's Horse-Man. Tauron is terrifying enough with his vicious hooves and deadly horns – but his creator Kensa has also armed him with a lethal two-pronged blade that can slice a man in half!

214

0	AGE
296	POWER
155	MAGIC LEVEL
88	FRIGHT FACTOR
281	SIZE

EVIL

DANGER DESTINY

Tauron is a master swordsman.

TECTON

THE ARMOURED GIANT

Tecton is an ancient Beast, once defeated by the White Knight of Forton. With four powerful legs, his body is covered in a thick hide of overlapping armour plates bristling with spikes. His short legs don't stop him from moving quickly – Tecton has a different method of chasing his prey. He can curl into a ball like a giant hedgehog and roll across the ground to crush his victims.

Tom defeated Tecton using an icicle-shaped diamond.

EVIL

T

AGE 323
POWER 208
MAGIC LEVEL 132
FRIGHT FACTOR 78
SIZE 304

TEMPRA

THE TIME STEALER

This slithering, one-eyed, tentacled Beast is not just capable of stealing souls – Tempra can also travel through time, changing history for ever!

218

DANGER DESTINY

Imagine everyone around you forgetting who you are, because time had been rewritten!

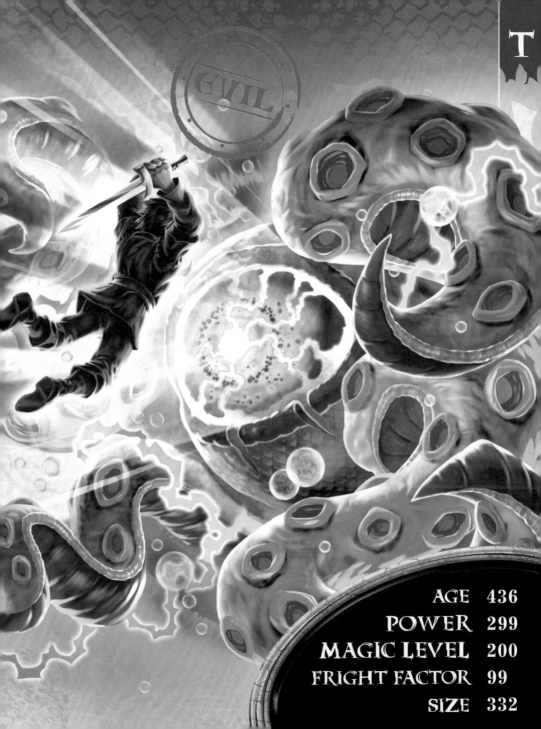

EVIL

AGE 436
POWER 299
MAGIC LEVEL 200
FRIGHT FACTOR 99
SIZE 332

TERRA

CURSE OF THE FOREST

The people of Kayonia have long told stories of a monstrous tree with the power to move through the forest: this is Terra. The Beast is covered in bark and moss, like a tree trunk. Indeed, he looks so much like a tree that many don't realise the danger they face until it's too late. When he attacks, his terrifying eyes emerge from beneath the bark and he reveals teeth like vicious splinters. He uses his branches to squeeze the life out of his victims.

EVIL

312	AGE
263	POWER
168	MAGIC LEVEL
72	FRIGHT FACTOR
260	SIZE

221

Terra turned animals and people alike into wood.

THORON

THE LIVING STORM

The guardian of one shard of the fabled Broken Star, which rests within its vaporous body, Thoron is a giant swirling cloud crackling with pulsing light, able to take a variety of forms. As Tom wondered during his battle with Thoron, how can you defeat a Beast you cannot touch?

420	AGE
250	POWER
181	MAGIC LEVEL
87	FRIGHT FACTOR
290	SIZE

GOOD

DANGER DESTINY

Whoever holds all four pieces of the Broken Star cannot be defeated!

TIKRON
THE JUNGLE MASTER

DANGER DESTINY

Tikron is a Good Beast but was put under a wicked spell by Kensa.

After laying eyes on this giant monkey Beast for the first time, an adventurer might try to back away to a "safe" distance – but that won't stop Tikron from bursting eardrums with his deafening screech. With his whip-like tail and terrible claws, Tikron is a ferocious opponent at both long and short range.

225

AGE	6
POWER	239
MAGIC LEVEL	156
FRIGHT FACTOR	87
SIZE	210

TOM

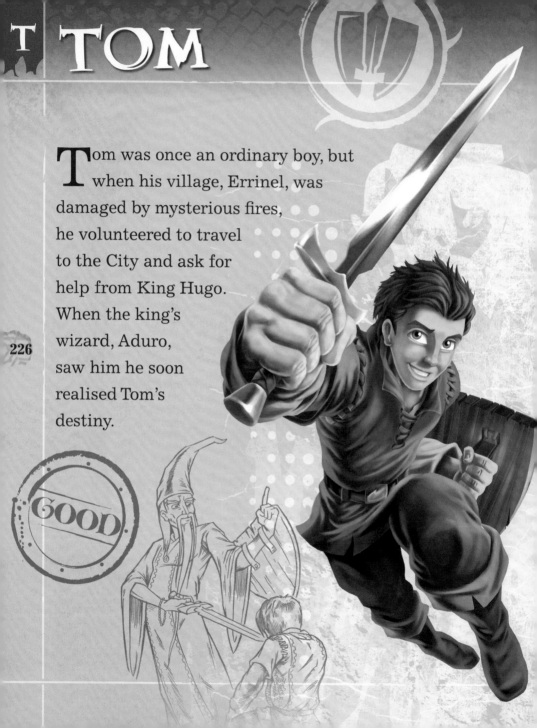

Tom was once an ordinary boy, but when his village, Errinel, was damaged by mysterious fires, he volunteered to travel to the City and ask for help from King Hugo. When the king's wizard, Aduro, saw him he soon realised Tom's destiny.

226

GOOD

As long as there is blood in his veins, Tom will continue his Beast Quests and do his best to protect the Kingdom of Avantia and all the known realms. Tom is armed with a sword given to him by Aduro, and his shield contains powerful tokens from the Good Beasts of Avantia.

227

DANGER DESTINY

Tom is the bravest boy in Avantia!

AGE	12
POWER	89
MAGIC LEVEL	132
FRIGHT FACTOR	74
SIZE	40

TORGOR

THE MINOTAUR

Torgor's thick, glistening coat of coal-black hair makes him almost impossible to spot in the night, though moonlight will pick out the two twisted horns that rise from his head. These horns are the key to Torgor's strength – removing them is the only way of defeating him...if you can get past his axe!

228

EVIL

224	AGE
210	POWER
126	MAGIC LEVEL
74	FRIGHT FACTOR
144	SIZE

229

Tom now wears Torgor's belt, which contains six jewels with magical powers.

DANGER • DESTINY

TORKA

THE SKY SNATCHER

This monstrous dragon-like Beast has talons sharp enough to shred stone, and three long, feathered necks each bearing the bald, wrinkled head of a carrion-eating bird.

EVIL

DANGER DESTINY

Each of Torka's beaks is big enough to swallow a cow!

AGE	81
POWER	240
MAGIC LEVEL	170
FRIGHT FACTOR	90
SIZE	318

TORNO
THE HURRICANE DRAGON

The violent winds that blow through the Northern Mountains are caused by Torno, one of the Beasts controlled by Sanpao the Pirate King. The Hurricane Dragon's foul breath is enough to blast his enemies through the air!

232

EVIL

256	AGE
267	POWER
181	MAGIC LEVEL
91	FRIGHT FACTOR
291	SIZE

233

DANGER ❖ DESTINY

Sanpao
once
controlled
Beasts using
magic from
the Tree of
Being.

TORPIX
THE TWISTING SERPENT

Torpix lives in the northwest of Seraph, among the dangerous mountains. He is the guardian of the Eternal Flame. His body is as long and thick as an oak tree, and his green and yellow scales are stronger than iron and covered with nasty spikes. His forked tongue can hurl yellow acid that melts through wood and metal.

GOOD

DANGER — DESTINY

Torpix sneaks up on his victims and squeezes the air from their bodies.

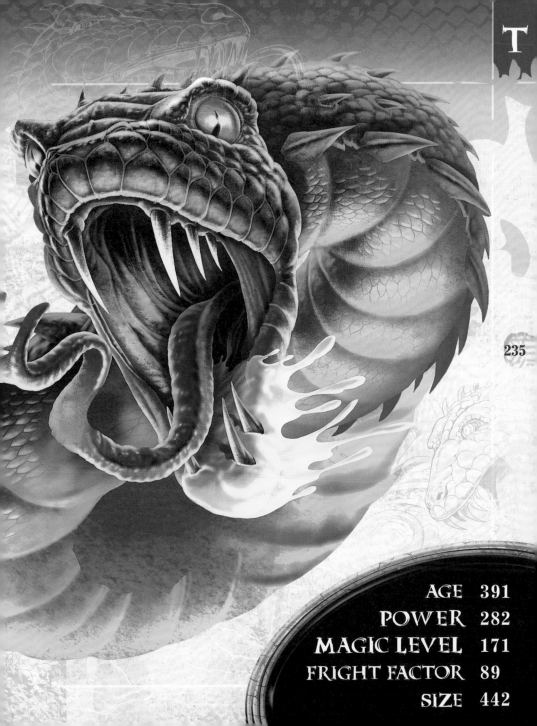

T

235

AGE	391
POWER	282
MAGIC LEVEL	171
FRIGHT FACTOR	89
SIZE	442

TREMA

THE EARTH LORD

Trema tunnels through the earth, using his sharp claws and jagged teeth to defeat enemies. His muscular body is covered in thick blue armour tough enough to withstand the strongest sword blows. His glowing red eyes help him see in the darkness and a row of jewels sparkles across his forehead.

236

406	AGE
178	POWER
178	MAGIC LEVEL
95	FRIGHT FACTOR
306	SIZE

TRILLION

THE THREE-HEADED LION

Trillion is armed with one tail for balance when jumping and running, three brains to plan his attack and four paws for movement and fighting. With claws that can slice through rocks and ninety teeth that can shatter bones, this is a mighty opponent!

EVIL

AGE	303
POWER	202
MAGIC LEVEL	193
FRIGHT FACTOR	85
SIZE	115

TUSK

THE MIGHTY MAMMOTH

Tusk's brown, shaggy hide covers a body taller than the tallest tree. This Beast bellows and roars with anger, so you know immediately when she is going to attack. Her victims can try to run for cover, but her trunk will ripple out like a snake to crush them. A drop of the slime from the Beast's golden tusks will send poison racing through their body and death is almost inevitable.

EVIL

238

DANGER · DESTINY

Tusk's enormous feet can squash her victims.

T

AGE	310
POWER	243
MAGIC LEVEL	161
FRIGHT FACTOR	70
SIZE	296

U URSUS

THE CLAWED ROAR

Like the other Beasts of Seraph, Ursus was not always so fearsome and brutal. He was once a gentle bear who protected the inhabitants of the forest, but he was turned evil by Malvel's cruel magic. This Beast terrifies his enemies with his deafening roar, dagger-like teeth and colossal claws.

240

172	AGE
271	POWER
179	MAGIC LEVEL
90	FRIGHT FACTOR
300	SIZE

DANGER DESTINY

Ursus can smell the fear of his prey.

VEDRA AND KRIMON
TWIN BEASTS OF AVANTIA

New Beasts of Avantia are born very rarely. Vedra and Krimon are twin baby dragons who share a special bond. They hatched from the same egg, which had lain hidden for centuries in the Nidrem Caves.

242

VEDRA

0	AGE
150	POWER
126	MAGIC LEVEL
50	FRIGHT FACTOR
120	SIZE

Because they are Good Beasts, they cannot attack – they can only protect. This meant that they were vulnerable to Malvel, the Dark Wizard.

DANGER DESTINY

Tom and Elenna rescued the dragons with help from Ferno and Epos.

243

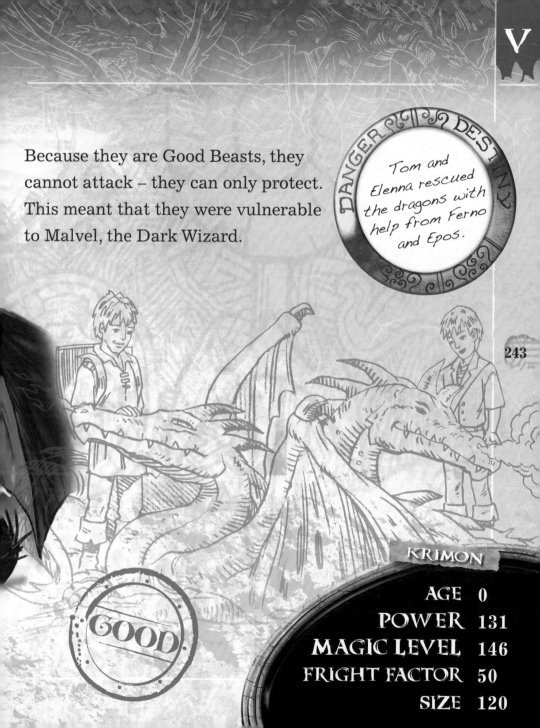

GOOD

KRIMON

AGE	0
POWER	131
MAGIC LEVEL	146
FRIGHT FACTOR	50
SIZE	120

VERAK

THE STORM KING

Tom and Elenna needed the help of their warrior friend, Amelia, to fend off this colossal lobster. He had been brought under the thrall of Kensa and Sanpao, to wreak havoc on the kingdom of Gwildor.

244

286	AGE
211	POWER
171	MAGIC LEVEL
94	FRIGHT FACTOR
337	SIZE

EVIL

VERMOK

THE SPITEFUL SCAVENGER

EVIL

246

377	AGE
253	POWER
138	MAGIC LEVEL
95	FRIGHT FACTOR
167	SIZE

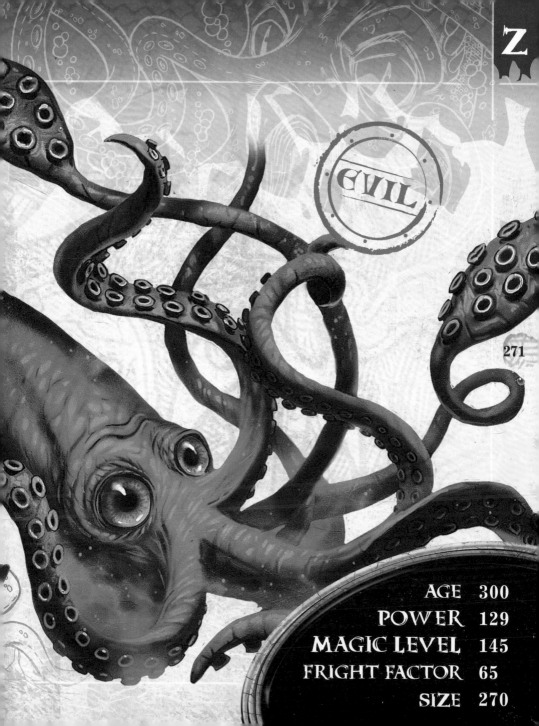

Z

EVIL

271

AGE	300
POWER	129
MAGIC LEVEL	145
FRIGHT FACTOR	65
SIZE	270

ZULOK
THE WINGED SPIRIT

At first glance, Zulok looks like a simple large bird with sharp talons and a wicked beak...and eyes that shine so bright any intruder is temporarily blinded. Though she does not seek a fight, she will protect her unborn young to the death – even if that means destroying honourable Questers like Tom and Elenna.

272

GOOD

211	AGE
249	POWER
157	MAGIC LEVEL
90	FRIGHT FACTOR
288	SIZE